A VERY BRAVE Witch

Alison McGHEE

Harry BLISS

A PAULA WISEMAN BOOK
Simon & Schuster Books for Young Readers
New York London Toronto Sydney

SIMON & SCHUSTER BOOKS FOR YOUNG READERS

An imprint of Simon & Schuster Children's Publishing Division

1230 Avenue of the Americas, New York, New York 10020

Text copyright © 2006 by Alison McGhee

Illustrations copyright © 2006 by Harry Bliss

First Simon & Schuster Books for Young Readers unjacketed hardcover edition August 2009

SIMON & SCHUSTER BOOKS FOR YOUNG READERS is a trademark of Simon & Schuster, Inc.

Also available in a Simon & Schuster Books for Young Readers jacketed hardcover edition.

Book design by Einav Aviram

Hand lettering by Paul Colin

The illustrations for this book are rendered in black ink and
watercolor on Arches 90 lb. watercolor paper.

Manufactured in China

2 4 6 8 10 9 7 5 3 1

The Library of Congress has cataloged a previous edition as follows:

McGhee, Alison, 1960–

A very brave witch / Alison McGhee ; illustrated by Harry Bliss. – 1st ed.

p. cm.

"A Paula Wiseman book."

Summary: A young witch describes what she does on Halloween, her favorite holiday.

ISBN: 978-0-689-86730-9 (hc)

[1. Halloween–Fiction. 2. Witches–Fiction.] I. Bliss, Harry, 1964– ill. II. Title.

PZ7.M4784675Ve 2006 [E]–dc22 2005016108

ISBN: 978-1-4169-8670-6 (unjacketed edition)

HAPPY
Halloween
Ruby

LOVE
Auntie
MARYANN
2010

To Holly McGhee—A. M.
For Charley and Ben Bliss—H. B.

Most humans do not wear pointy hats.

Humans are rarely known to cackle.

HA. HA,
HA. HA

Nothing too bad, except, you know... the green thing.